This Little Tiger book belongs to:

_____

_____

_____

LITTLE TIGER PRESS LTD, an imprint of the Little Tiger Group

1 Coda Studios, 189 Munster Road, London SW6 6AW · www.littletiger.co.uk

First published in Great Britain 2012 · This edition published 2017

Text copyright © Steve Smallman 2012 · Illustrations copyright © Cee Biscoe 2012

Steve Smallman and Cee Biscoe have asserted their rights to be identified as the author and illustrator of this work

under the Copyright, Designs and Patents Act, 1988 · All rights reserved

Printed in China · LTP/1400/2159/1217 · 10 9 8 7 6 5 4 3 2 1 · ISBN 978-1-84869-840-6

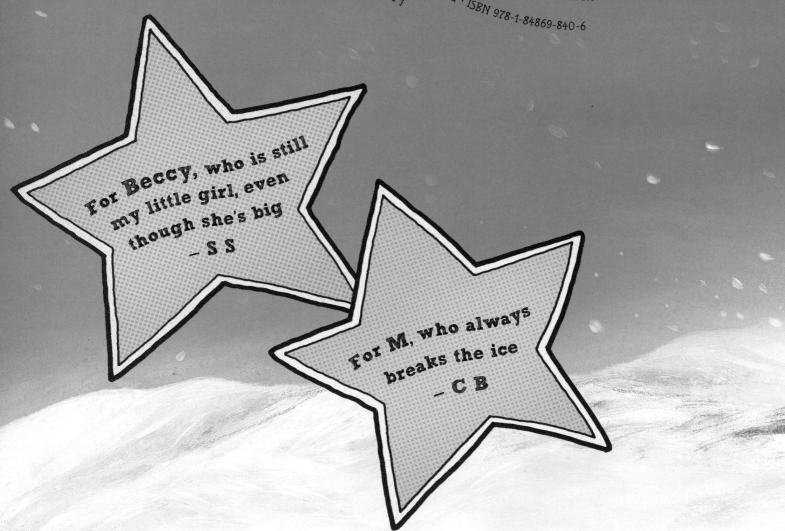

For Beccy, who is still
my little girl, even
though she's big
— S S

For M, who always
breaks the ice
— C B

# SUPER★PANTS!

by Steve Smallman

Illustrated by Cee Biscoe

LITTLE TIGER

LONDON

It was Christmas day. Mummy,
Daddy and little Lola polar bear
were opening their presents.
Mummy had a lovely scarf.
Lola had SUPERHERO PANTS!

"Look!" she cried. "I'm Super Lola polar bear!"

"You look fantastic!" smiled Daddy. "Now, what could MY present be?"

# "Superhero pants?!

I didn't think these came
in my size?" said Daddy.

"They **don't**," replied Mummy.
"I made them just for YOU! There's a cape too."

"Now we're **both** superheroes in our super pants!" cried Lola. "Let's go and rescue something!"

"Off you go, Super Daddy!" chuckled Mummy. "See you later."

Super Lola polar bear raced off,
looking for adventure!

Super Daddy lumbered after her
with his cape flapping in the breeze.

"I'm on top of the world!"

she shouted.

"Be careful, Lola," said Daddy.

But Lola wasn't listening.
She was too busy being
the **best** superhero **ever**.

"And I'm super **loud** toooo!"

she yelled.

"You certainly are!"
said Daddy.
But Lola was off again . . .

"Daddy, that birdie's
stuck!" gasped Lola.
"Let's rescue him!"

"Squawk!"

She
scrambled
up to
reach,

and the puffin
flew off.

"Hooray! We did it,
Daddy!" cheered Lola.
"Let's go and help
someone else!"

After a very busy morning, Daddy sat down
for a rest. It was hard work being a superhero!

"Daddy, look!" cried Lola.

"Those penguins are floating out to sea!

Let's rescue them!"

"Erm, I don't think . . ." replied Daddy,
but it was too late.

"Lola!"
shouted Daddy.
"Slow down!"

As Lola tripped, Super Daddy
did a super leap and
caught her just in time.

"I'm flying!" laughed Lola, as they skidded down the hill.

But Daddy couldn't stop...

"Super Lola to the

They shot off the cliff with a WHOOSH, and flew straight towards the penguins.

rescue!" she yelled.

# ASH!

Daddy and Lola landed on the ice and eight grumpy penguins sploshed into the water!

"Oops! Sorry!"

said Daddy.

"Don't worry, penguins," cried Lola.
"We've come to save you! My daddy will
carry you on his back. Won't you, Daddy?"
"Yes," sighed Daddy. "Why not?"

Back on shore, Daddy dried the penguins
with his superhero cape.
"Are you all right?" he asked.
The penguins weren't sure.

"Would a little Christmas dinner make you
feel better?" asked Daddy.
The penguins were sure that it would.

By now it was getting dark,
and little Lola was feeling a bit tired, so Daddy
wrapped her up and gave her a big cuddle.
"Let's go home," he said.

Mummy said it was a lovely surprise to have so many new friends for Christmas dinner. "Have you had a super time?" she asked. "Oh yes, Mummy, it's been my best Christmas ever!" said Lola. "Me and my Daddy are the **greatest superheroes** in the **whole wide world!**"

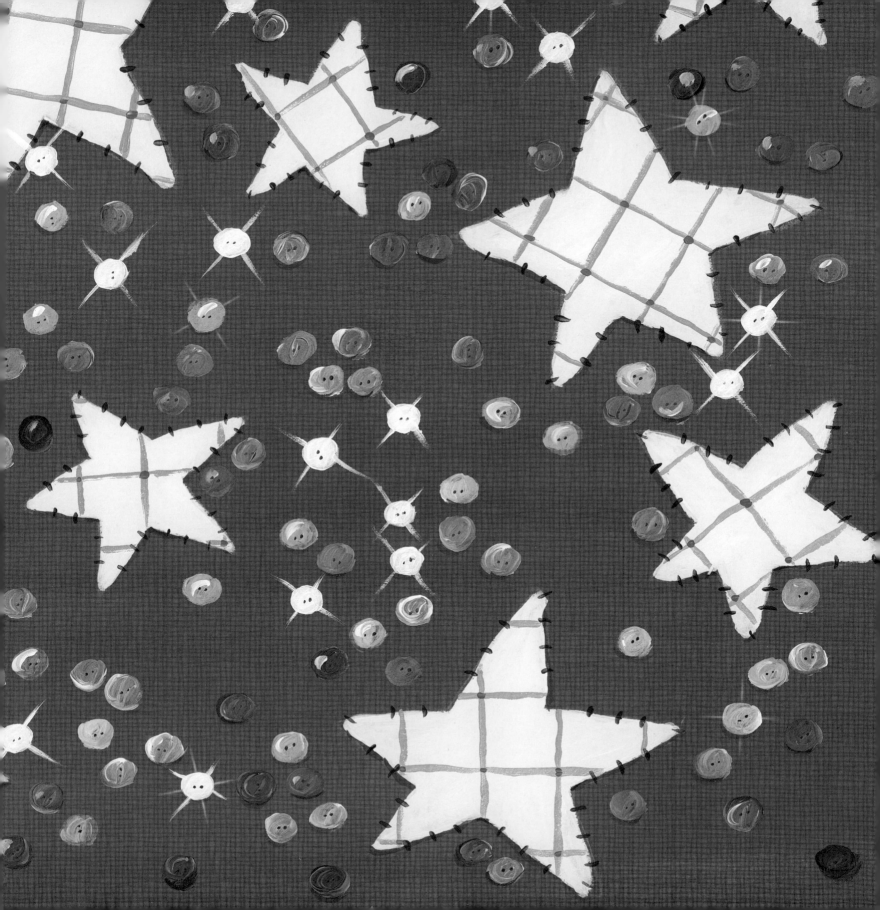